A Voyage in Everyday Words :
NATURE

Jeremy and Sara Walenn

A Voyage in Everyday Words

讓孩子走進生活，
用眼睛、耳朵及聯想力學習英語生活詞彙

你有否發現孩子在英語造句或作文時，連很常見的事物的意思也不懂表達呢？若是如此，你應該意識到，孩子迫切需要擴展生活詞彙量，提升最基本的英語溝通能力了。但是，孩子應該學些甚麼詞彙？要學多少詞彙？怎樣學才是有效的方法呢？

語言是重要的溝通工具，因此，學語言也不應該脫離生活的環境。對孩子而言，學習日常碰到及熟悉的事物的詞彙，除了有助他們理解和記憶之外，還能引發他們學習的興趣。而孩子學好了生活詞彙，他們的英語溝通能力便能大大提升！

A Voyage in Everyday Words 系列，是以嶄新的方法幫助孩子輕鬆學習英語生活詞彙的套裝。每套書由 "詞彙學習書" 及 "發音光碟" 組合而成，圍繞Cooking (煮食)、Nature (自然)、Home and Friends (家庭和朋友)、Sports and Games (運動和遊戲)、Festival (節慶) 及 Shopping and Entertainment (購物和娛樂) 六大生活主題，教導孩子 3000 個在日常生活中會碰到的常用詞彙。作者 Jeremy and Sara Walenn 具有30年教授以英語作為第二語言的人士的經驗，他們在本套裝中特別為華人小孩子挑選了最應該學懂的生活詞彙。因此，你的孩子將能熟悉西方的生活情景，又能學習到最地道的英語！

在生活情景中學習常見事物的名稱

翻閱本書，孩子將會看到一個個與主題相關的生活情景，並從中學習常見事物的名稱、詞彙和詞組。孩子可以輕輕鬆鬆學會最該學懂的生活詞彙。

利用詞彙地圖（Word Map）的概念，用聯想力學習新詞彙

除了主題詞彙，本書亦延伸選取了更多相關詞彙，着重從 "詞的相近組合" 及 "詞的相關主題" 兩大方面，幫助孩子以聯想力學習更多新詞彙。本書以有趣的詞彙地圖編排，表示詞彙的延伸關係，並配以色彩繽紛的插圖，能夠有效激起孩子學習的興趣。

讓孩子邊聽邊學標準的英語發音

書內所有詞彙和例句，都是由作者親自錄音。作者標準的英語發音，將有助於改善孩子的英語發音。左頁下方的曲目編號，對應光碟音檔的首兩個號碼，方便查找之餘，也方便選聽個別生字。

家長不妨與孩子一起翻閱本書，透過角色扮演，以生動活潑的方式學習詞彙。家長還可以與孩子一同聯想出更多的詞彙，繼續擴展孩子的詞彙量呢！

資深英籍教師，
為孩子挑選最應該認識的生活詞彙

JEREMY WALENN

Jeremy Walenn graduated in Law then taught in primary schools for five years before becoming a teacher of English as a Foreign Language. He was a Director of Studies in the UK and Head of Languages at a UK university. He has been a senior examiner for international examination boards and examined in the Far East, Europe and South America. He is now working for a UK ELT publisher.

He has written EFL text books, including academic, examination and young learners' material. He is the author of *Passport to the Cambridge Proficiency Examination* (Macmillan) and the *Talking Trinity* series.

SARA WALENN

Sara Walenn began teaching English as a Foreign Language (EFL) in 1978. She is a teacher trainer, EFL author and examiner. She was a Director of Studies in the UK and is now working for a UK EFL publisher in Asia.

韋倫先生

韋倫先生擁有超過30年教導以英語作為第二語言的人士學習英語的經驗，曾於英國擔任教務長，任大學的語言中心主管。韋倫先生除了擁有豐富的教學經驗外，也是歐美及遠東多個國際考試評核局的資深考官，現為英國的出版社撰寫ELT書籍。

韋倫先生曾撰寫一系列有關準備英語國際考試的出版物，當中包括 *Passport to the Cambridge Proficiency Examination* (Macmillan) 及 the *Talking Trinity* series (Garnet publications) 等。

韋倫女士

韋倫女士自1978年開始教授以英語作為外語 (English as a Foreign Language) 的課程，了解非以英語作為母語的人士學習英語的需要。在教學之餘，她致力於培訓英語教師，並擔任EFL課程的作者和考官。韋倫女士現時於英國擔任教務長並為英國的出版社撰寫ELT書籍。

The Voyage Route 漫遊路徑

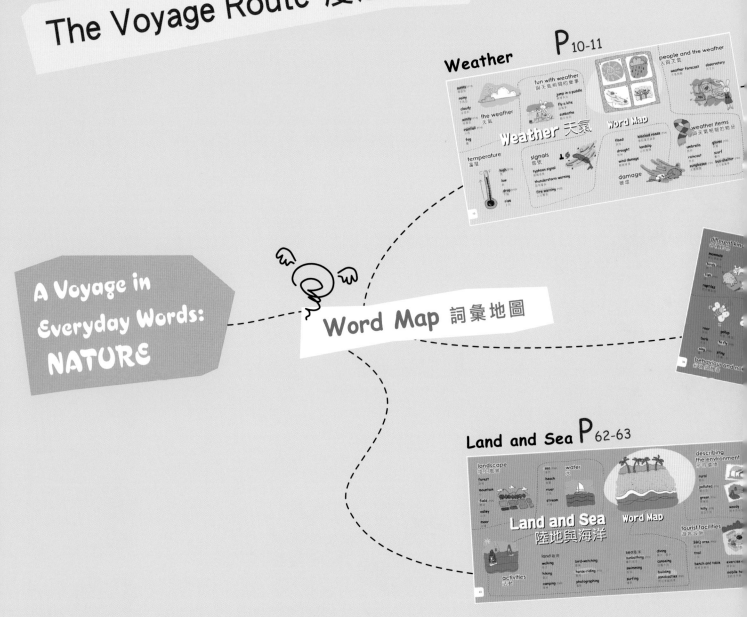

A Voyage in Everyday Words: NATURE

Word Map 詞彙地圖

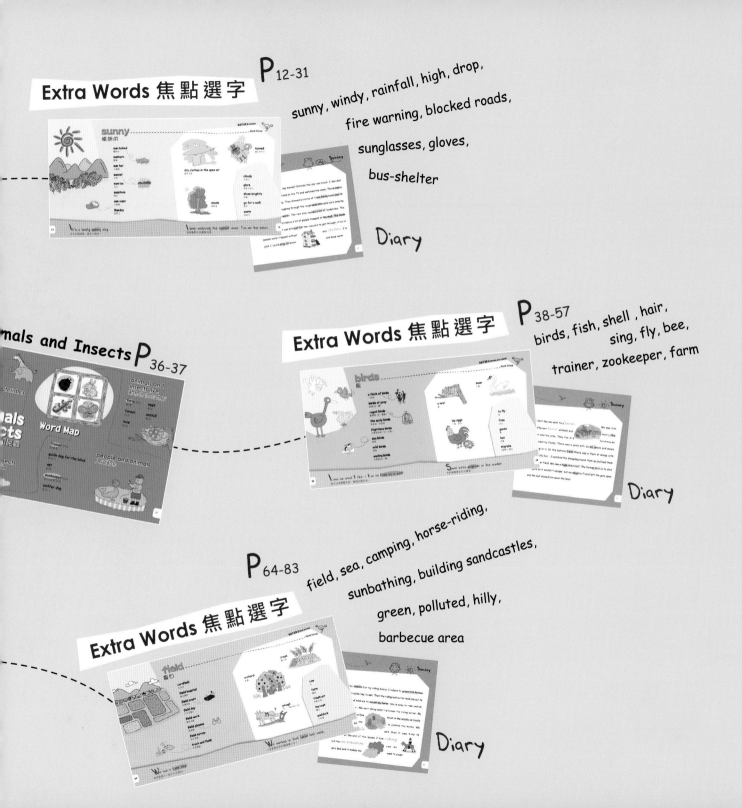

Extra Words 焦點選字

Diary

Animals and Insects P36-37

Extra Words 焦點選字

Diary

Extra Words 焦點選字

Diary

Chapter One
Weather

sunny (P12)
晴朗的

rainy
下雨的

cloudy
多雲的

windy (P14)
刮風的

the weather
天氣

rainfall (P16)
下雨

fog
霧

fun with weather
與天氣相關的樂事

jump in a puddle
跳進水洼

fly a kite
放風箏

sunbathe
曬日光浴

Weather 天氣

temperature
溫度

high (P18)
高

low
低

drop (P20)
下降

rise
上升

signals
信號

typhoon signal
颱風信號

thunderstorm warning
雷雨警告

fire warning (P22)
火災警報

people and the weather
人與天氣

weather forecast
天氣預報

observatory
天文台

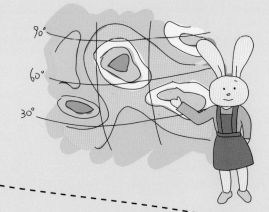

Word Map

flood
洪水

blocked road (P24)
被堵塞的道路

drought
乾旱

landslide
山泥傾瀉

wind damage
颱風破壞

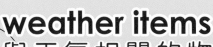

weather items
與天氣相關的物品

umbrella
雨傘

gloves (P28)
手套

raincoat
雨衣

scarf
圍巾

sunglasses (P26)
太陽眼鏡

bus-shelter (P30)
巴士候車亭

damage
破壞

sunny
晴朗的

sun-baked
曬乾的

sunburn
曬傷

sun hat
太陽帽

sunset
日落

sunrise
日出

sunshine
陽光

sun visor
太陽帽

Sunday
星期日

It's a lovely sunny day.
今天天氣晴朗，真令人愉快。

Word Group

dry clothes in the open air
曬晾衣服

tanned
曬成棕色的

cloudy
多雲的

glare
刺眼的強光

shine brightly
照耀

shade
陰暗處

go for a walk
散步

warm
溫暖的

I love watching the sunset when I'm on the beach.
我很喜歡在海灘看日落。

windy
刮風的

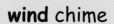

wind chime
風鈴

strong wind
大風

tail wind
順風

window
窗

windmill
風車

windless
無風

windfall
被風吹落的果實

wind down
放鬆一下

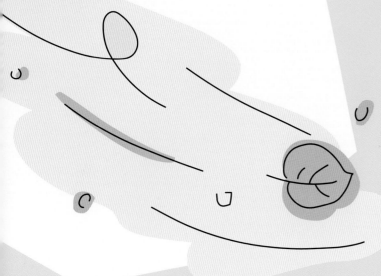

It's windy enough today to fly a kite!
今天的風大得可以放風箏了！

blow out a candle
吹蠟燭

fan
扇子

blowy
有風的

typhoon
颱風

tornado
龍捲風

cool
涼爽的

rainy
下雨的；多雨的

a tree bent by the wind
被風吹得歪斜的樹

High winds made the ferry trip very unpleasant.
因為刮大風，這次的水上之旅很不順利。

rainfall
下雨

driving rain
狂吹猛打的雨

raindrops
雨點

rain cloud
雨雲

rain off
因雨中斷(或延期)

rainbow
彩虹

rain water
雨水

raincoat
雨衣

the **rain**y season
雨季

I got soaked in the rain.
我被雨水淋得全身濕透了。

flood
洪水

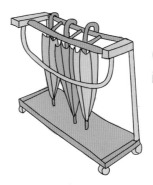

umbrella stand
雨傘架

wet
濕

bucket
水桶

slippery floor
濕漉漉的地板

shelter
躲避處

soaked
濕透

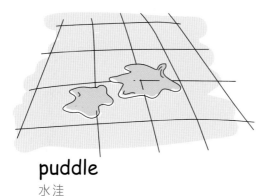

puddle
水洼

The tennis match was rained off.
網球比賽因下雨而中斷。

17

high
高

high heels
高跟鞋

high jump
跳高

high chair
兒童坐的高腳椅

high level
高級

high temperature
高溫

high and low
四處

high-rise building
高樓大廈

high speed
高速；急速

The train is going at a high speed.
火車正在高速行駛。

tower
塔

bird's-eye view
鳥瞰

cable car
纜車

lift
升降機

roof
屋頂

tree top
樹頂

observation tower
瞭望台

Ferris wheel
摩天輪

I looked high and low for my glasses, but I couldn't find them anywhere. 我四處找我的眼鏡，可就是找不到。

drop
下降

YESTERDAY

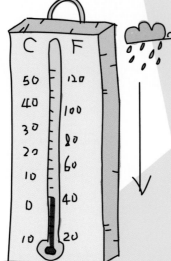

TODAY

a sharp drop
急劇下跌；暴跌

drop off
讓(某人)下車

drop behind
落伍

drop by
順道拜訪

droplet
小滴

droppings
鳥獸的糞便

drop a hint
給予暗示、提示

drop a clanger
衝口而出說了令人不快的話

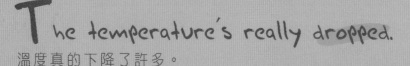

The temperature's really dropped.
溫度真的下降了許多。

download
下載

fall
跌倒

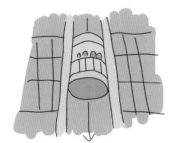

the lift is going down
升降機正在往下

throw
拋擲

bounce
彈；拍（球）

collapse
倒下

lost
失去

tumble
絆倒

Could you drop me off in town?
你能讓我在城中下車嗎？

fire warning
火災警報

fire fighter
消防員

fire engine
消防車

fire
火

firework
煙花

fire alarm
火災警報；火災警報器

fire door
防煙門

catch **fire**
着火

set **fire** to something
放火燒（某東西）

Careful! The kitchen's going to catch fire!
小心，廚房快要着火了！

Word Group

flame
火焰

smoke
煙

tap
水龍頭

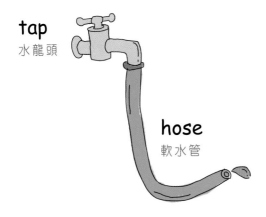

hose
軟水管

burn
燃燒

dust
灰燼

grill
烤

spark
火花

We always watch fireworks at Chinese New Year.
每年春節我們都會去看煙花表演。

blocked roads
被堵塞的道路

a block
積木

a block of flats
住宅大廈

block letters/capitals
大寫

road block
路障

block a view
阻擋景觀

road
道路

road sign
路標

roadside stand
路邊攤檔

We can't go any further – the road's blocked.
路被堵塞了，我們不能繼續前進了。

landslide
山泥傾瀉

traffic jam
交通擠塞

block of ice
大塊冰

trees
樹木

wait
等候

rescuer
救援人員

disconnected
中斷的；沒有聯繫的

rocks
巨石

Please write your name and address in block capitals.
請用大寫字體填寫你的姓名和地址。

sunglasses

太陽眼鏡

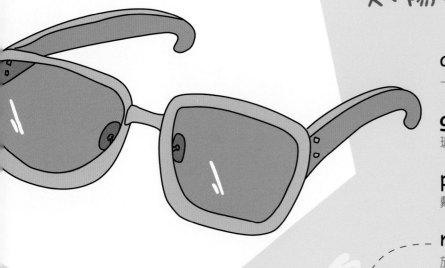

a pair of sunglasses
一副太陽眼鏡

glass
玻璃杯

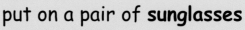

put on a pair of sunglasses
戴上一副太陽眼鏡

magnifying glass
放大鏡

sun hat
太陽帽

sunglasses case
太陽眼鏡盒

safety glasses
護目鏡

pose in sunglasses
戴上太陽眼鏡擺姿勢

09 I want a glass of water, please.
請給我一杯水。

.Word Group

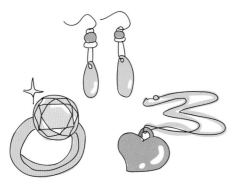

accessories
裝飾品；小配件

cap
鴨舌帽

optician
眼鏡店

fashion
時尚

film stars
電影明星

shiny
光亮的

summer
夏季

protect the eyes
保護眼睛

She usually wears sunglasses when she drives.
她總是配戴着太陽眼鏡駕車。

gloves

手套

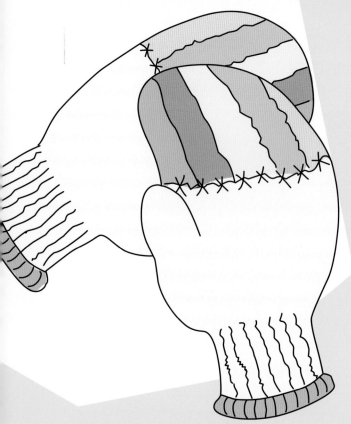

a pair of **gloves**
一對手套

boxing **gloves**
拳擊手套

baseball **glove**
棒球手套

glove puppet
手套式玩偶

oven **gloves**
焗爐手套

rubber **gloves**
膠手套

put on a pair of **gloves**
穿上手套

take off **gloves**
脫下手套

 10

Put your gloves on.
請你穿戴上手套。

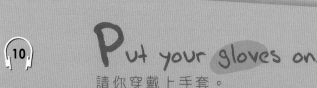

mittens
連指手套

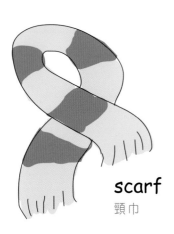

scarf
頸巾

bare hands
徒手（做某事情）

frostbite
凍傷

keep warm
保持溫暖

pockets
口袋

protect
保護

winter
冬季

I'm glad I've got warm gloves - it's so cold today.
今天真是寒冷，幸好我穿戴了手套。

29

bus-shelter
巴士候車亭

bus stop
巴士站

bus driver
巴士司機

bus number
巴士號碼

bus lane
巴士專用線

get on a **bus**
登上巴士

school **bus**
校巴

sheltered
被遮蔽的

wait for a **bus**
等候巴士

The heavy fog upset our timetable for the trip.
濃霧耽誤了我們的行程。

ticket machine
售票機

timetable
時間表

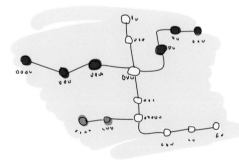

advertisement
廣告

double-decker
雙層巴士

fare
車費

queue
排隊

terminus
終點站

route
路線

We queued up for the bus.
我們排隊候車。

31

Saturday

A beautiful day. The sun shone in through my bedroom window. I called

my friend and we decided to go to the beach. We met each other at the

bus stop. We were both wearing the same designer *glasses* .

We looked really cool!! We didn't have to wait long for

the bus. It was a double-decker, so we sat upstairs. We had a great time.

The temperature soared so we put on our sun hats and lay on

sun-baked sand. On our way back, we heard lots of sirens and

then were overtaken by fire engines. The heat had caused a

forest fire. The fire engines *blocked the*

road and it took ages to get home.

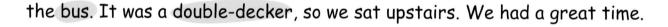

What a difference a day makes!! Outside the sky was black. I decided not to go out. I switched on the TV and watched the news. There was a typhoon 8 on the way. They showed pictures of trees being bent over in the wind, ferries ploughing through the rough seas and cable cars swaying backwards and forwards. The rain also caused a lot of landslides. The fire brigade had to rescue a lot of people trapped in the mud. The roads were blocked so it was difficult for the rescuers to get through. A lot of people were trapped without any *shelter*. I'm glad I could stay at home and keep warm.

Chapter Two

Animals and Insects

different kinds of animals
各種動物

mammals
哺乳類動物

birds (P38)
鳥

fish (P40)
魚

reptiles
爬行類動物

fur
軟毛

shell (P42)
外殼

pouch
(袋鼠的)育兒袋

whiskers
鬚

hair (P44)
毛髮

antenna
昆蟲的觸鬚

characteristics
特徵

Animals and Insects
動物和昆蟲

roar
吼叫

gallop
疾馳(馬匹)

bark
吠叫

fly (P48)
飛

sing (P46)
唱

sting
(蚊蟲)叮

behaviour and noises
行為與聲音

bee (P50)
蜜蜂

ladybird
瓢蟲

butterfly
蝴蝶

ant
螞蟻

insects
昆蟲

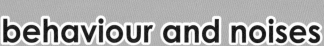

Word Map

where animals and insects live
動物居住的地方

farm (P56)
農場

nest
鳥巢

forest
森林

anthill
蟻窩

hive
蜂巢

trainer (P52)
訓練員

guide dog for the blind
導盲犬

vet
獸醫

zookeeper (P54)
動物園管理員

sniffer dog
嗅探犬

people and animals
人與動物

birds
鳥

a flock of birds
一群鳥

birds of prey
猛禽(如：鷹)

caged birds
觀賞鳥（如：鸚鵡）

the early bird
早起者；早到者

flightless birds
不會飛的鳥（如：企鵝）

sea birds
海鳥

wild birds
野鳥

wading birds
涉禽類(如：鶴)

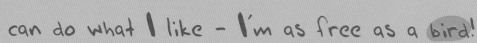

I can do what I like - I'm as free as a bird!
我可以做喜歡的事，像鳥兒般自由。

swan
天鵝

nest
巢

lay eggs
下蛋；產卵

fly
飛

free
自由

goose
鵝

hen
母雞

migrate
(鳥類的)遷徙

Some birds migrate in the winter.
有些鳥類會在冬天遷徙。

39

fish

魚

fishing rod
釣魚竿

fishing boat
漁船

fish fillet
魚柳

fish pond
魚塘

fish and chips
炸魚和薯條

fisherman
漁民；漁夫

fish around
四處摸索；探聽

jelly **fish**
水母

I fished around my bag for my keys.
我在手袋裏尋找鎖匙。

Word Group

whale
鯨

mermaid
美人魚

deep sea
深海；遠洋

penguin
企鵝

swimming
游泳

seaweed
海草

shrimp
蝦

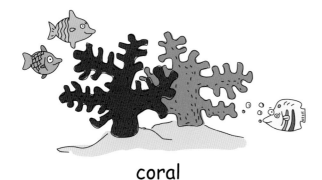

coral
珊瑚

I went fishing by the river with my dad.
我和爸爸去河邊釣魚。

41

shell

外殼

seashell
貝殼

snail **shell**
蝸牛殼

eggshell
蛋殼

crab **shell**
蟹殼

coconut **shell**
椰殼

shell necklace
貝殼項鏈

come out of your **shell**
形容害羞的人變得活躍起來

tortoise **shell**
龜殼

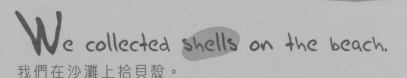

We collected shells on the beach.
我們在沙灘上拾貝殼。

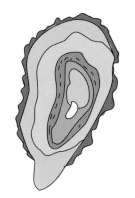

oyster
蠔

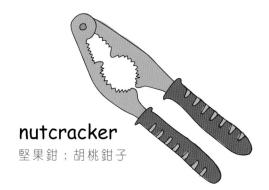

nutcracker
堅果鉗；胡桃鉗子

almond
杏仁

beach
海灘

chestnut
栗子

hard
堅硬的

nuts
堅果；果仁

pearl
珍珠

I made a shell necklace for my sister.
我為妹妹做了一條貝殼項鏈。

hair

毛髮

coarse hair
粗髮

hair cut
理髮

hair stylist
髮型設計師

hair clip
髮夾

hair gel
造型啫喱；髮膠

hairy
多毛的

thin hair
稀少的頭髮

thick hair
濃密的頭髮

My cat's got long hair.
我的貓兒長了一身長毛。

.Word Group

comb
梳子

scissors
剪刀

Alice band
髮箍

conditioner
護髮素

mirror
鏡子

soft
柔軟的

shampoo
洗髮水

wig
假髮

shaver
剃鬚刀

You should have your hair cut today.
你今天得去理髮了。

sing

唱

sing softly
柔和地唱

sing loudly
大聲地唱

sing up
更用力地唱

sing along
唱和

sing out
大聲叫喊

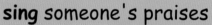

sing someone's praises
讚揚某人

singer
歌手

singer-song writer
創作歌手

singing
歌唱

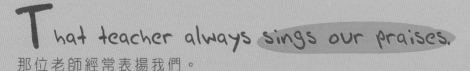

That teacher always sings our praises.
那位老師經常表揚我們。

mic
麥克風

live band
現場樂隊

songbook
歌曲集

karaoke
卡拉OK

melody
旋律

performance
表演

hum a tune
輕哼曲調

sing off-key
唱走調

She sang the baby to sleep.
她唱着歌哄嬰兒入睡。

fly

飛

a fly
蒼蠅

butterfly
蝴蝶

dragonfly
蜻蜓

flyover
天橋

flying saucer
飛碟

fly a flag
升旗；懸掛旗幟

fly a plane
駕駛飛機

time flies
時間飛逝

🎧19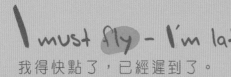

I must fly - I'm late!
我得快點了，已經遲到了。

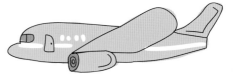

plane
飛機

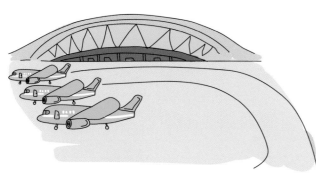

airport
飛機場

wings
翅膀；翼

bird
鳥

balloon
氣球

trapeze artist
高空秋千表演者

sky
天空

wind
風

Time flies when you're having fun.
快樂不知時日過。

bee
蜜蜂

as busy as a bee
極忙碌

beehive
蜂窩；蜂箱

beekeeper
養蜂人

beeline
直線

bee sting
被蜂螫的痛楚

honey**bee**
蜜蜂

queen **bee**
蜂后

spelling **bee**
拼字比賽會

🔊 20

A swarm of bees flew into the garden.
一群蜜蜂飛進了花園。

make honey
釀蜜

swarm
蜂群

buzz
嗡嗡聲

dangerous
危險的

flower
花

hard-working
努力工作的

sting
螫；刺

butterfly
蝴蝶

My arm swelled where the bee stung me.
我的手臂被蜜蜂螫了以後，腫起來了。

trainer
訓練員

a **train** set
一套模型鐵路(玩具)

animal **trainer**
動物訓練員

personal **trainer**
私人教練

train
訓練

train of events
一連串事件

training shoes
運動鞋

trainee
受訓者

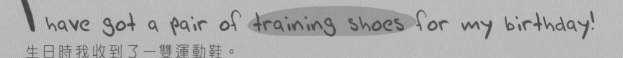

I have got a pair of training shoes for my birthday!
生日時我收到了一雙運動鞋。

punish
懲罰

coach
教練

learn
學習

license
執照

practise
練習

praise
稱讚；讚美

try
嘗試

teacher
老師

I want to be a dolphin trainer when I grow up.
長大後，我想做一名海豚訓練員。

zookeeper
動物園管理員

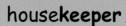

goalkeeper
守門員

housekeeper
傭人；管家

keep fit
保持健康

keep up
維持

keep on doing something
繼續做某事

keep my word
守信

keep track
追蹤（進度、情況等）

shopkeeper
店主

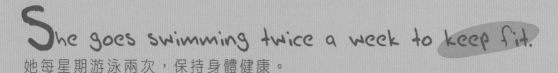

She goes swimming twice a week to keep fit.
她每星期游泳兩次，保持身體健康。

.Word Group

gate
大門；閘門

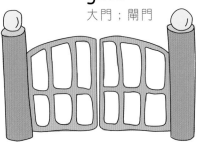

feed the animals
餵動物

souvenirs
紀念品

opening hours
營業時間

rule
規章準則

security
安全

ticket
門票

theme park
主題公園

Let's meet at the school gate tomorrow morning.
明天早上，我們在學校大門前見。

farm
農場

dairy farm
乳製品農場

fish farm
養魚場

farm machinery
農業機器

farm worker
農場工人

farmer
農夫；農場主人

organic farm
有機農場

poultry farm
家禽農場

wind farm
有許多風車的農場

What kind of farm is this?
這是哪一種農場？

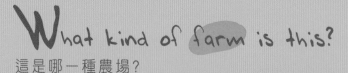

Word Group

crop
農作物；莊稼

vegetable
蔬菜

scarecrow
稻草人

animals
動物

fresh
新鮮的

fruit
水果

rural area
鄉郊；農村

green
綠色

hard-working
努力工作的

hunt
打獵

My mum always buys fruit from an organic farm.
我媽媽經常去有機農場買水果。

Saturday

I went to a nature reserve with my friends last weekend. There were all kinds of local animals and *birds* there, including sea birds, wading birds and wild birds I sometimes see in the garden. We learnt about the different birdsongs - some *birds sing* beautifully, some cheep and some, like parrots, even speak! We saw nests made of twigs and mud and birds'eggs - all different colours and sizes. We saw honeybees buzzing in and out of the beehives and the beekeeper let us try some honey from the honeycomb. The aquarium was decorated with *shells,* such as mother-of-pearl and we saw a shark.

The next day we went to a *farm*. We saw lots of different *farm* animals and met the farmer and his wife. They live in a farmhouse surrounded by fields. There was a pond with ducks, geese and swans swimming in it. In the bottom field, there was a flock of sheep with thick, woolly hair. I watched the sheepdog round them up and lead them into another field. We saw a huge, black bull. The farmer told us to shut the gate so it wouldn't escape, but my naughty friend left the gate open and the bull chased him down the lane!

59

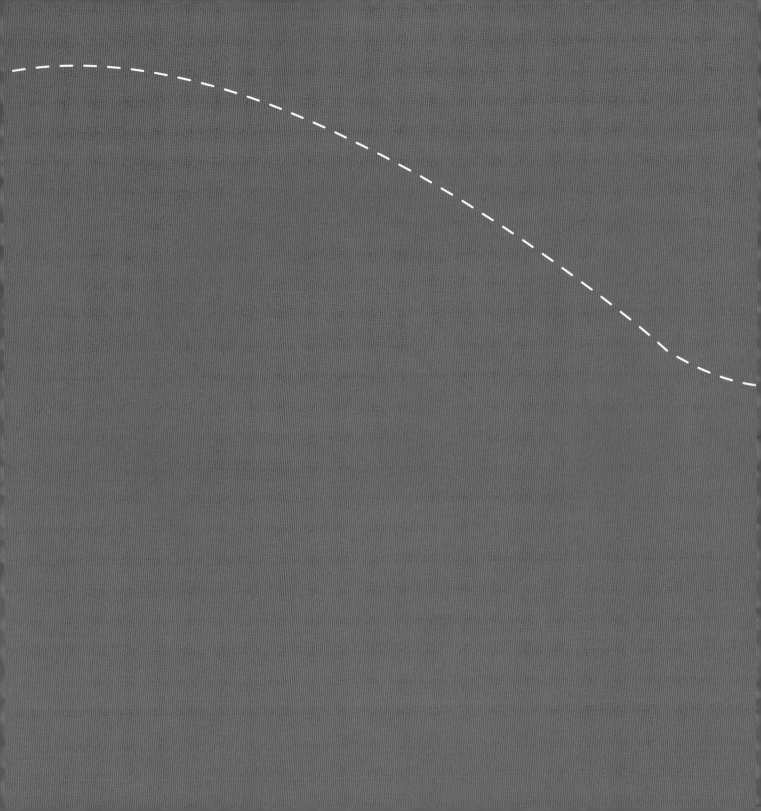

Chapter Three
Land and Sea

landscape
陸上風景

forest
森林

mountain
山

field (P64)
農田

valley
山谷

moor
沼澤

sea (P66)
海洋

beach
海灘

river
河流

stream
小溪

water
水

Land and Sea
陸地與海洋

activities
活動

land 陸地

walking
散步

hiking
遠足

camping (P68)
露營

bird-watching
(在大自然中) 觀察研究野鳥

horse-riding (P70)
騎馬

photography
攝影

25

describing
the environment
形容環境

rural
鄉郊

green (P76)
青蔥的

polluted (P78)
被污染

hilly (P80)
多山丘的

woody
樹木茂密的

Word Map

tourist facilities
遊客設施

sea 海洋

sunbathing (P72)
曬日光浴

swimming
游泳

surfing
滑浪

diving
潛水；跳水

canoeing
伐獨木舟

**building
sandcastles** (P74)
用沙堆砌城堡

barbecue area (P82)
燒烤區

trail
小徑

bench and table
長椅及桌子

exercise areas
健身區

mobile toilet
流動洗手間

63

field

農田

cornfield
玉米田

field hospital
戰地醫院

field event
田賽項目

field day
戶外活動日

field-work
實地考察

field glasses
望遠鏡

field survey
野外考察

track and **field**
田徑運動

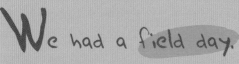

We had a field day.
我們度過了一個戶外活動日。

.Word Group

crop
農作物；莊稼

orchard
果園

plough
犁（一種耕種工具）

cow
牛

farm
農場

fresh air
新鮮空氣

harvest
豐收

paddock
小牧場

We worked in that farm last week.
上個星期我們在農場裏工作。

sea

海洋

high seas
公海；深海領域

sea lane
海上航道

seasickness
暈船

seafood
海鮮

sea breeze
海風

sea level
水平線

sea bird
海鳥

sea-front
海濱

The pirates attacked ships on the high seas.
海盜在公海上襲擊了船隻。

Word Group

fishing
釣魚

wave
海浪

liner
郵輪

deep
深

ocean
海洋

sailing
航海

tide
潮水

wide
廣闊的

Eating seafood is good for you.
吃海鮮對你的身體有益。

camping ...
露營

camp out
露營

campsite
營地

camp beds
露營用的可折疊式睡床

camping stove
野外用的爐具

campstool
摺椅

campfire
營火；營火會

go camping
去露營

scout camp
童子軍營

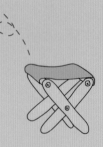

I go camping every year with my family.
我們一家每年都去露營。

.....Word Group

tent
帳篷

water carrier
隨身攜帶的水壺

sleeping bag
睡袋

backpack
背包

groundsheet
(露營時鋪地用的)防潮布

pitch a tent
搭帳篷

take down a tent
拆帳篷

wild
野外

We camped out under the stars last summer.
去年夏天，我們去野外露營。

horse-riding
騎馬

groom a horse
餵馬

horse
馬

horseshoe
馬蹄鐵

horse race
賽馬

horse rider
騎師

horse show
馬術表演

fall off a horse
從馬上掉下來

horse around
搗蛋；胡鬧

I schooled this pony myself.
這匹小馬是由我訓練的。

Word Group

mount
騎上

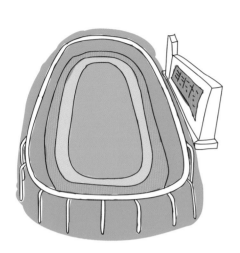

racecourse
跑馬場

dressage
馴馬技術

gallop
飛馳

pony
小馬

stable
馬廄

jump
跳躍

ponytail
馬尾辮子

The jump was too high so the horse refused.
這個障礙太高了，馬兒不肯跳過去。

sunbathing
曬日光浴

sunflower
向日葵

sunbeam
太陽光線

sunshine
陽光

sun-dried
曬乾的（如：乾果）

sun block
太陽油

sundeck
（建築物或游泳池等的）日光浴處

sunglasses
太陽眼鏡

sunburn
曬傷皮膚

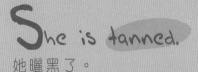

She is tanned.
她曬黑了。

Word Group

pool
泳池

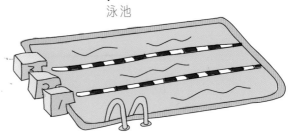

go brown
變成棕色

drinks
飲料

swimming
游泳

tan
曬黑；曬成褐色

burn
曬傷

peel
(皮膚曬傷)剝落

beach
海灘

She goes swimming every week.
她每個星期都去游泳。

73

building sandcastles
用沙堆砌城堡

build up
興建；建造

build a fire
生火

build on **sand**
建立在不穩固的基礎上

building site
建築工地

high-rise **building**
高樓大廈

a **builder**
建築者

sandal
涼鞋

sandy
多沙的

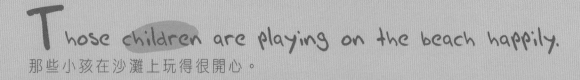

Those children are playing on the beach happily.
那些小孩在沙灘上玩得很開心。

Word Group

swimwear
游泳衣

seashells
貝殼

bucket
水桶

children
兒童

spade
鏟子

stone
石頭

sea water
海水

tide
潮水

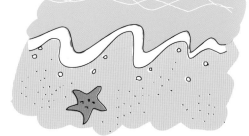

I need to buy a set of swimwear before I go to Hawaii this summer. 今年夏天去夏威夷之前，我要買一套游泳衣。

75

green

青蔥的

green salad
蔬菜沙律

green tea
綠茶

green vegetable
青菜；蔬菜

greengrocer
菜販；蔬菜水果商

greenhouse
溫室

green light
綠燈

greenness
綠色；未成熟

green man
綠色行人信號燈

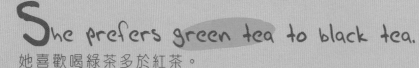

She prefers green tea to black tea.
她喜歡喝綠茶多於紅茶。

leaves
樹葉

golf
高爾夫球運動

colour
顏色

environmentally friendly
環保的

fresh
新鮮的

pasture
牧場

new
新的

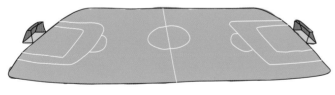

pitch
球場

The green vegetables are really fresh.
這些青菜很新鮮。

polluted ....
被污染

air pollution
空氣污染

acid-rain pollution
酸雨污染

light pollution
光污染

noise pollution
噪音污染

pollute
污染

polluter
污染者

pollutant
污染物

water pollution
水質污染

The air pollution is really serious in this city.
這個城市的空氣污染很嚴重。

.Word Group

smelly
臭的

factory waste
工業廢料

smoggy
煙霧彌漫的

eco-friendly
環保的

greenhouse effect
溫室效應

infected
被感染的

stained
玷污的

sick
不舒服的

The greenhouse effect is changing the climate every year. 溫室效應令每年的天氣產生變化。

hilly
多山丘的

anthill
蟻丘;蟻塚

foothill
位於山腳位置的小山丘

hillside
山坡

hilltop
山頂

hillock
小丘

rolling hills
(坡度較緩的)小山

the top of the hill
山頂

uphill
向上的;上坡的

The old man lives on the top of the hill.
這位老人住在山頂上。

hiking
爬山

steep slope
很陡峭的斜度

banks
河岸；湖岸

gentle slope
輕微的斜度

highlands
高地

high
高的

slope
斜面；斜坡

valley
山谷

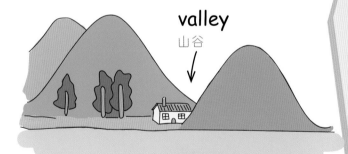

In the story, the children lived "over the hills and far away". 這個故事裏的孩子們是住在遙遠的山那邊。

barbecue (BBQ) area
燒烤區

a barbecue
燒烤

barbecue sauce
燒烤醬

barbecued pork
叉燒

barbecue site
燒烤場地

barbecue fish
燒魚

light a **barbecue**
在燒烤爐生火

have a **BBQ** in the garden
在花園裏燒烤

get the **BBQ** going
繼續燒烤

Do you fancy coming to a barbecue?
你喜歡參加野外燒烤嗎？

grill
燒烤架

charcoal
木炭

firelighters
打火機

bake
烤；烘(麵包、蛋糕等)

char-grilled
炭燒的

kebabs
肉串

skewers
烤肉用的叉子

salt
鹽

Put it on the grill for few more minutes.
把這個放在架上再多烤幾分鐘。

Thursday

I went on a *camping* trip with my class. I packed my **tent** and sleeping bag and we set off with our teacher. We had to climb a **steep hill** to get to the campsite. We pitched our tent and I put down the groundsheet. The campsite was in a beautiful *green field*. We were all hungry so we decided to have a *barbecue*. Our teacher took us to the barbecue site put in some firelighters and covered them with charcoal.

The *barbecue* got going quite quickly and we all helped to put pieces of **pork** and **green vegetables** on **skewers** and **grill** them. The smell of the char-grilled food was delicious. I drank some water from my water carrier. After we had eaten we all sat and watched a beautiful sunset.

I went to the stables for my riding lesson. I helped to groom the horses and gave them some hay to eat. Then the riding instructor took me out to the paddock and told me to mount my horse. She is easy to ride and we set off at a canter. We went along some trails near the riding school. My instructor taught me how  to sit in the saddle correctly and how to use the reins to control the horse. We galloped across a *field* and then it was time to dismount at the end of the lesson. I love *riding* but the *air pollution* can be very bad and it makes me want to cough.

Series Name ： A Voyage in Everyday Words
Book Name ： A Voyage in Everyday Words: NATURE
Authors ： Jeremy and Sara Walenn
Editor ： Leung Ho Yan
Published by ： The Commercial Press (H.K.) Ltd.
8/F, Eastern Central Plaza, 3 Yiu Hing Road, Shau Kei Wan, Hong Kong
http://www.commercialpress.com.hk
Distributed by ： SUP Publishing Logistics (HK) Limited
3/F, C & C Building, 36 Ting Lai Road, Tai Po, N.T., Hong Kong
Printed by ： C & C Offset Printing Co., Ltd.
C & C Building, 36 Ting Lai Road, Tai Po, N.T., Hong Kong
Edition ： First Edition, September 2010
© 2010 The Commercial Press (Hong Kong) Ltd.
ISBN 978 962 07 1917 2
Printed in Hong Kong

系列名：A Voyage in Everyday Words

書名：A Voyage in Everyday Words: NATURE

作者：Jeremy and Sara Walenn

責任編輯：梁可茵

出版：商務印書館 (香港) 有限公司

香港筲箕灣耀興道3號東滙廣場8樓

http://www.commercialpress.com.hk

發行：香港聯合書刊物流有限公司

香港新界大埔汀麗路36號中華商務印刷大廈3字樓

印刷：中華商務彩色印刷有限公司

香港新界大埔汀麗路36號中華商務印刷大廈

版次：2010年9月第1次印刷

© 2010 商務印書館 (香港) 有限公司

ISBN 978 962 07 1917 2

Printed in Hong Kong